WE ARE SUCH STUFF
AS DREAMS ARE MADE ON
AND OUR LITTLE LIFE IS
ROUNDED WITH A
SLEEP

Designed by Archie Lieberman

Editorial preparation by
Nai Y. Chang and Dirk Luykx

Library of Congress Catalogue
Card Number: 77-16022

ISBN 0-8109-1325-9
ISBN 0-8109-2150-2 pbk.

The Publishers wish to thank
Ballantine Books, New York,
for typographical assistance.

All the photographs in this book were
made with a Nikon F camera with
a Vivitar 20mm f3.8 lens;
film was Kodak Tri-X, rated at ASA 400;
available lighting

Published in 1978 by
Harry N. Abrams, B.V., The Netherlands

Printed and bound in Japan

THE MUMMIES OF GUANAJUATO

INSTITUTO MEXICANO PARA
LA INFANCIA Y LA FAMILIA

MUSEO DE LAS MOMIAS

BONO DE COOPERACION PARA
ESCUELAS DE LENTO APRENDIZAJE

GUANAJUATO

$ 3.00 D N° 26886

Photography / Archie Lieberman   Story / Ray Bradbury

Harry N. Abrams, Inc., Publishers, New York

Preface

I WENT to Guanajuato, Mexico, to see the town and to photograph its famous mummies.

Before I came into the city I made a picture of the road from the car window as I drove from San Miguel de Allende. You drive these roads over barren countryside and over mountains and then—whack!—there is a classic European city coming up out of nowhere. I made some snapshots around the town square, of people in the street, of the Juarez Theatre.

And then I was in the long hall lined with glass-fronted specimen cases that hold the mummies. With a camera up to my eye I can witness almost anything. I began making pictures hoping that there was no curse on what I was doing and that I was not disturbing the spirits of the dead. I rationalized that since there was a charge of a few pesos to see the mummies, this was their job. It was like paying to see a freak show at a carnival. But these were fleeting thoughts. As I worked, others came.

I was reminded of Henry Moore's remark about the ruins of ancient buildings: "When architecture is unusable, it inevitably becomes aesthetically the same as sculpture." I also pictured the richness of Georges Rouault's India ink brushstrokes in his series of engravings *Miserere*. When I saw the mummies I thought of Moore and Rouault and the new sculptural exploration of the human figure done in ceramic and plastic and metal. For me, photographing the mummies could have been a study in line, form, texture and tone except that I could not escape the reality that what I was photographing had once lived.

After I left Mexico I was reminded that Ray Bradbury had written a story about the mummies some thirty years before. I read it again. At one point in it, the American tourist Joseph says of the mummies, "I'd like a color shot of each...it would be an amazing, an ironical book to publish. The more you think, the more it grows on you." It grew on me.

I put the pictures and text together. The coincidence of the works going so well together was curious and frightening—as if transcendent forces wanted it that way.

To the next in line, whoever it may be.

Archie Lieberman

NEXT IN LINE
NEXT IN LINE
NEXT IN LINE
NEXT IN LINE

THE NEXT IN LINE
THE NEXT IN LINE
THE NEXT IN LINE
THE NEXT IN LINE
THE NEXT IN LINE
THE NEXT IN LINE
THE NEXT IN LINE
THE NEXT IN LINE

Ray Bradbury

IT WAS a little caricature of a town square. In it were the following fresh ingredients: a candy-box of a bandstand where men stood on Thursday and Sunday nights exploding music; fine, green-patinated bronze-copper benches all scrolled and flourished; fine blue and pink tiled walks—blue as women's newly lacquered eyes, pink as women's hidden wonders; and fine French-clipped trees in the shapes of exact hatboxes. The whole, from your hotel window, had the fresh ingratiation and unbelievable fantasy one might expect of a French villa in the nineties. But no, this was Mexico! and this a plaza in a small colonial Mexican town, with a fine State Opera House (in which movies were shown for two pesos admission: *Rasputin and the Empress, The Big House, Madame Curie, Love Affair, Mama Loves Papa*).

Joseph came out on the sun-heated balcony in the morning and knelt by the grille, pointing his little box Brownie. Behind him, in the bath, the water was running and Marie's voice came out:

"What're you doing?"

He muttered "—a picture." She asked again. He clicked the shutter, stood up, wound the spool inside, squinting, and said, "Took a picture of the town square. God, didn't those men shout last night? I didn't sleep until two-thirty. We would have to arrive when the local Rotary's having its whirgding."

"What're our plans for today?" she asked.

"We're going to see the mummies," he said.

"Oh," she said. There was a long silence.

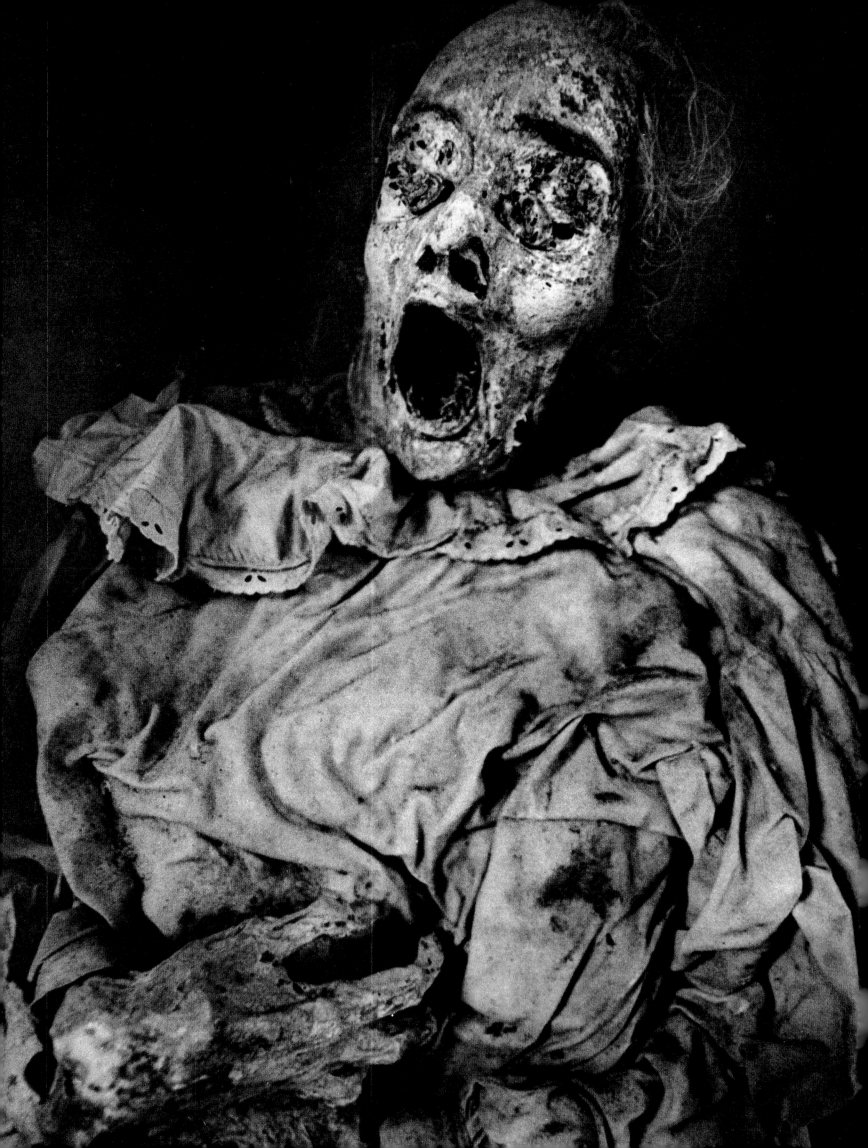

He came in, set the camera down, and lit himself a cigarette.

"I'll go up and see them alone," he said, "if you'd rather."

"No," she said, not very loud. "I'll go along. But I wish we could forget the whole thing. It's such a lovely little town."

"Look here!" he cried, catching a movement from the corner of his eyes. He hurried to the balcony, stood there, his cigarette smoking and forgotten in his fingers. "Come quick, Marie!"

"I'm drying myself," she said.

"Please, hurry," he said, fascinated, looking down into the street.

There was movement behind him, and then the odor of soap and water-rinsed flesh, wet towel, fresh cologne; Marie was at his elbow. "Stay right there," she cautioned him, "so I can look without exposing myself. I'm stark. What *is* it?"

"Look!" he cried.

A procession traveled along the street. One man led it, with a package on his head. Behind him came women in black rebozos, chewing away the peels of oranges and spitting them on the cobbles; little children at their elbows, men ahead of them. Some ate sugar cane, gnawing away at the outer bark until it split down and they pulled it off in great hunks to get at the succulent pulp, and the juicy sinews on which to suck. In all, there were fifty people.

"Joe," said Marie behind him, holding his arm.

It was no ordinary package the first man in the procession carried on his head, balanced delicately as a chicken-plume. It was covered with silver satin and silver fringe and silver rosettes. And he held it gently with one brown hand, the other hand swinging free.

This was a funeral and the little package was a coffin.

Joseph glanced at his wife.

She was the color of fine, fresh milk. The pink color of the bath was gone. Her heart had sucked it all down to some hidden vacuum in her. She held fast to the french doorway and watched the traveling people go, watched them eat fruit, heard them talk gently, laugh gently. She forgot she was naked.

He said, "Some little girl or boy gone to a happier place."

"Where are they taking—her?"

She did not think it unusual, her choice of the feminine pronoun. Already she had identified herself with that tiny fragment parceled like an unripe variety of fruit. Now, in this moment, she was being carried up the hill within compressing darkness, a stone in a peach, silent and terrified, the touch of the father against the coffin material outside; gentle and noiseless and firm inside.

"To the graveyard, naturally; that's where they're taking her," he said, the cigarette making a filter of smoke across his casual face.

"Not *the* graveyard?"

"There's only one cemetery in these towns, you know that. They usually hurry it. That little girl had probably been dead only a few hours."

"A few hours———"

She turned away, quite ridiculous, quite naked, with only the towel supported by her limp, untrying hands. She walked toward the bed. "A few hours ago she was alive, and now———"

He went on, "Now they're hurrying her up the hill. The climate isn't kind to the dead. It's hot, there's no embalming. They have to finish it quickly."

"But to *that* graveyard, that horrible place," she said, with a voice from a dream.

"Oh, the mummies," he said. "Don't let that bother you."

She sat on the bed, again and again stroking the towel laid across her lap. Her eyes were blind as the brown paps of her breasts. She did not see him or the room. She knew that if he snapped his fingers or coughed, she wouldn't even look up.

"They were eating fruit at her funeral, and laughing," she said.

"It's a long climb to the cemetery."

She shuddered, a convulsive motion, like a fish trying to free itself from a deep-swallowed hook. She lay back and he looked at her as one examines a poor sculpture; all criticism, all quiet and easy and uncaring. She wondered idly just how much his hands had had to do with the broadening and flattening and changement of her body. Certainly this was not the body he'd started with. It was past saving now. Like clay which the sculptor has carelessly impregnated with water, it was impossible to shape again. In order to shape clay you warm it with your hands, evaporate the moisture with heat. But there was no more of that fine summer weather between them. There was no warmth to bake away the aging moisture that collected and made pendant now her breasts and body. When the heat is gone, it is marvelous and unsettling to see how quickly a vessel stores self-destroying water in its cells.

"I don't feel well," she said. She lay there, thinking it over. "I don't feel well," she said again, when he made no response. After another minute or two she lifted herself. "Let's not stay here another night, Joe."

"But it's a wonderful town."

"Yes, but we've seen everything." She got up. She knew what came next. Gayness, blitheness, encouragement, everything quite false and hopeful. "We could go on to Patzcuaro. Make it in no time. You won't have to pack, I'll do it all myself, darling! We can get a room at the Don Posada there. They say it's a beautiful little town—"

"This," he remarked, "is a beautiful little town."

"Bougainvillea climb all over the buildings—" she said.

"These—" he pointed to some flowers at the window "—are bougainvillea."

"—and we'd fish, you like fishing," she said in bright haste. "And I'd fish, too, I'd learn, yes I would, I've always *wanted* to learn! And they say the Tarascan Indians there are almost Mongoloid in feature, and don't speak much Spanish, and from there we could go to Paracutin, that's near Uruapan, and they have some of the finest lacquered boxes there, oh, it'll be fun, Joe. I'll pack. You just take it easy, and—"

"Marie."

He stopped her with one word as she ran to the bathroom door.

"Yes?"

"I thought you said you didn't feel well?"

"I didn't. I don't. But, thinking of all those swell places—"

"We haven't seen one-tenth of this town," he explained logically. "There's that statue of Morelos on the hill, I want a shot of that, and some of that French architecture up the street . . . we've traveled three hundred miles and we've been here one day and now want to rush off somewhere else. I've already paid the rent for another night. . . ."

"You can get it back," she said.

"Why do you want to run away?" he said, looking at her with an attentive simplicity. "Don't you like the town?"

"I simply adore it," she said, her cheeks white, smiling. "It's so green and pretty."

"Well, then," he said. "Another day. You'll love it. That's settled."

She started to speak.

"Yes?" he asked.

"Nothing."

She closed the bathroom door. Behind it she rattled open a medicine box. Water rushed into a tumbler. She was taking something for her stomach.

He came to the bathroom door.

"Marie, the mummies don't bother you, do they?"

"Unh-unh," she said.

"Was it the funeral, then?"

"Unh."

"Because, if you were really afraid, I'd pack in a moment, you know that, darling."

He waited.

"No, I'm not afraid," she said.

"Good girl," he said.

The graveyard was enclosed by a thick adobe wall, and at its four corners small stone angels tilted out on stony wings, their grimy heads capped with bird droppings, their hands gifted with amulets of the same substance, their faces unquestionably freckled.

In the warm smooth flow of sunlight which was like a depthless, tideless river, Joseph and Marie climbed up the hill, their shadows slanting blue behind them. Helping one another, they made the cemetery gate, swung back the Spanish blue iron grille and entered.

It was several mornings after the celebratory fiesta of El Dia de Muerte, the Day of the Dead, and ribbons and ravels of tissue and sparkle-tape still clung like insane hair to the raised stones, to the hand-carved, love-polished crucifixes, and to the above-ground tombs which resembled marble jewel-cases. There were statues frozen in angelic postures over gravel mounds, and intricately carved stones tall as men with angels spilling all down their rims, and tombs as big and ridiculous as beds put out to dry in the sun after some nocturnal accident. And within the four walls of the yard, inserted into square mouths and slots, were coffins, walled in, plated in by marble plates and plaster, upon which names were struck and upon which hung tin pictures, cheap peso portraits of the inserted dead. Thumb-tacked to the different pictures were trinkets they'd loved in life, silver charms, silver arms, legs, bodies, silver cups, silver dogs, silver church medallions, bits of red crape and blue ribbon. On some places were painted slats of tin showing the dead rising to heaven in oil-tinted angels' arms.

Looking at the graves again, they saw the remnants of the death fiesta. The little tablets of tallow splashed over the stones by the lighted festive candles, the wilted orchid blossoms lying like crushed red-purple tarantulas against the milky stones, some of them looking horridly sexual, limp and withered. There were loop-frames of cactus leaves, bamboo, reeds, and wild, dead morning-glories. There were circles of gardenias and sprigs of bougainvillea, desiccated. The entire floor of the yard seemed a ballroom after a wild dancing, from which the participants have fled; the tables askew, confetti, candles, ribbons and deep dreams left behind.

They stood, Marie and Joseph, in the warm silent yard, among the stones, between the walls. Far over in one corner a little man with high cheekbones, the milk color of the Spanish infiltration, thick glasses, a black coat, a gray hat and gray, unpressed pants and neatly laced shoes, moved about among the stones, supervising something or other that another man in overalls was doing to a grave with a shovel. The little man with glasses carried a thrice folded newspaper under his left arm and had his hands in his pockets.

"*Buenos diaz, senora y senor!*" he said, when he finally noticed Joseph and Marie and came to see them.

"Is this the place of *las momias?*" asked Joseph. "They do exist, do they not?"

"*Si,* the mummies," said the man. "They exist and are here. In the catacombs."

"*Por favor,*" said Joseph. "*Yo quiero veo las momias, si?*"

"*Si, senor.*"

"*Me Espanol es mucho estupido, es muy malo,*" apologized Joseph.

"No, no, *senor*. You speak well! This way, please."

He led between the flowered stones to a tomb near the wall shadows. It was a large flat tomb, flush with the gravel, with a thin kindling door flat on it, padlocked. It was unlocked and the wooden door flung back rattling to one side. Revealed was a round hole the circled interior of which contained steps which screwed into the earth.

Before Joseph could move, his wife had set her foot on the first step. "Here," he said. "Me first."

"No. That's all right," she said, and went down and around in a darkening spiral until the earth vanished her. She moved carefully, for the steps were hardly enough to contain a child's feet. It got dark and she heard the caretaker stepping after her, at her ears, and then it got light again. They stepped out into a long whitewashed hall twenty feet under the earth, dimly lit by a few small gothic windows high in the arched ceiling. The hall was fifty yards long, ending on the left in a double door in which were set tall crystal panes and a sign forbidding entrance. On the right end of the hall was a large stack of white rods and round white stones.

"The soldiers who fought for Father Morelos," said the caretaker.

They walked to the vast pile. They were neatly put in

place, bone on bone, like firewood, and on top was a mound of a thousand dry skulls.

"I don't mind skulls and bones," said Marie. "There's nothing even vaguely human to them. I'm not scared of skulls and bones. They're like something insectile. If a child was raised and didn't know he had a skeleton in him, he wouldn't think anything of bones, would he? That's how it is with me. Everything human has been scraped off *these*. There's nothing familiar left to be horrible. In order for a thing to be horrible it has to suffer a change you can recognize. This isn't changed. They're still skeletons, like they always were. The part that changed is gone, and so there's nothing to show for it. Isn't that interesting?"

Joseph nodded.

She was quite brave now.

"Well," she said, "let's see the mummies."

"Here, *senora*," said the caretaker.

He took them far down the hall away from the stack of bones and when Joseph paid him a peso he unlocked the forbidden crystal doors and opened them wide and they looked into an even longer, dimly lighted hall in which stood the people.

They waited inside the door in a long line under the arch-roofed ceiling, fifty-five of them against one wall, on the left, fifty-five of them against the right wall, and five of them way down at the very end.

"Mister Interlocutor!" said Joseph, briskly.

They resembled nothing more than those preliminary erections of a sculptor, the wire frame, the first tendons of clay, the muscles, and a thin lacquer of skin. They were unfinished, all one hundred and fifteen of them.

They were parchment-colored and the skin was stretched as if to dry, from bone to bone. The bodies were intact, only the watery humors had evaporated from them.

"The climate," said the caretaker. "It preserves them. Very dry."

"How long have they been here?" asked Joseph.

"Some one year, some five, *senor,* some ten, some seventy."

There was an embarrassment of horror. You started with the first man on your right, hooked and wired upright against the wall, and he was not good to look upon, and you went on to the woman next to him who was unbelievable and then to a man who was horrendous and then to a woman who was very sorry she was dead and in such a place as this.

"What are they doing here?" said Joseph.

"Their relatives did not pay the rent upon their graves."

"Is there a rent?"

"*Si, senor.* Twenty pesos a year. Or, if they desire the permanent interment, one hundred seventy pesos. But our people, they are very poor, as you must know, and one hundred seventy pesos is as much as many of them make in two years. So they carry their dead here and place them into the earth for one year, and the twenty pesos are paid, with fine intentions of paying each year and each year, but each year and each year after the first year they have a burro to buy or a new mouth to feed, or maybe three new mouths, and the dead, after all, are not hungry, and the dead, after all, can pull no ploughs; or there is a new wife or there is a roof in need of mending, and the dead, remember, càn be in no beds with a man, and the dead, you understand, can keep no rain off one, and so it is that the dead are not paid up upon their rent."

"*Then* what happens? Are you listening, Marie?" said Joseph.

Marie counted the bodies. One, two, three, four, five, six, seven, eight, "What?" she said, quietly.

"Are you listening?"

"I think so. What? Oh, yes! I'm listening."

Eight, nine, ten, eleven, twelve, thirteen.

"Well, then," said the little man. "I call a *trabajando* and with his delicate shovel at the end of the first year he does dig and dig and dig down. How deep do you think we dig, *senor?*"

"Six feet. That's the usual depth."

"Ah, no, ah, no. There, senor, you would be wrong.

Knowing that after the first year the rent is liable not to be paid, we bury the poorest two feet down. It is less work, you understand? Of course, we must judge by the family who own a body. Some of them we bury sometimes three, sometimes four feet deep, sometimes five, sometimes six, depending on how rich the family is, depending on what the chances are we won't have to dig him from out his place a year later. And, let me tell you, *senor,* when we bury a man the whole six feet deep we are very certain of his staying. We have never dug up a six-foot-buried one yet, that is the accuracy with which we know the money of the people."

Twenty-one, twenty-two, twenty-three. Marie's lips moved with a small whisper.

"And the bodies which are dug up are placed down here against the wall, with the other *compañeros.*"

"Do the relatives know the bodies are here?"

"Si." The small man pointed. "This one, *yo veo?*" It is new. It has been here but one year. His *madre y padre* know him to be here. But have they money? Ah, no."

"Isn't that rather gruesome for his parents?"

The little man was earnest. "They never think of it," he said.

"Did you hear that, Marie?"

"What?" Thirty, thirty-one, thirty-two, thirty-three, thirty-four. "Yes. They never think of it."

"What if the rent is paid again, after a lapse?" inquired Joseph.

"In that time," said the caretaker, "the bodies are reburied for as many years as are paid."

"Sounds like blackmail," said Joseph.

The little man shrugged, hands in pockets. "We must live."

"You are certain no one can pay the one hundred seventy pesos all at once," said Joseph. "So in this way you get them for twenty pesos a year, year after year, for maybe thirty years. If they don't pay, you threaten to stand *mamacita* or little *nino* in the catacomb."

"We must live," said the little man.

Fifty-one, fifty-two, fifty-three.

Marie counted in the center of the long corridor, the standing dead on all sides of her.

They were screaming.

They looked as if they had leaped, snapped upright in their graves, clutched hands over their shriveled bosoms and screamed, jaws wide, tongues out, nostrils flared.

And been frozen that way.

All of them had open mouths. Theirs was a perpetual screaming. They were dead and they knew it. In every raw fiber and evaporated organ they knew it.

She stood listening to them scream.

They say dogs hear sounds humans never hear, sounds so many decibels higher than normal hearing that they seem nonexistent.

The corridor swarmed with screams. Screams poured from terror-yawned lips and dry tongues, screams you couldn't hear because they were so high.

Joseph walked up to one standing body.

"Say 'ah,' " he said.

Sixty-five, sixty-six, sixty-seven, counted Marie, among the screams.

"Here is an interesting one," said the proprietor.

They saw a woman with arms flung to her head, mouth wide, teeth intact, whose hair was wildly flourished, long and shimmery on her head. Her eyes were small pale white-blue eggs in her skull.

"Sometimes, this happens. This woman, she is a cataleptic. One day she falls down upon the earth, but is really not dead, for, deep in her, the little drum of her heart beats and beats, so dim one cannot hear. So she was buried in the graveyard in a fine inexpensive box. . . ."

"Didn't you know she was cataleptic?"

"Her sisters knew. But this time they thought her at last dead. And funerals are hasty things in this warm town."

"She was buried a few hours after her 'death?' "

"*Si,* the same. All of this, as you see her here, we would never have known, if a year later her sisters, having other things to buy, had not refused the rent on her burial. So we dug very quietly down and loosed the box and took it up and opened the top of her box and laid it aside and looked in upon her———"

Marie stared.

This woman had wakened under the earth. She had torn, shrieked, clubbed at the box-lid with fists, died of suffocation, in this attitude, hands flung over her gaping face, horror-eyed, hair wild.

"Be pleased, *senor,* to find that difference between *her* hands and these other ones," said the caretaker. "Their peaceful fingers at their hips, quiet as little roses. Hers? Ah, hers! are jumped up, very wildly, as if to pound the lid free!"

"Couldn't rigor mortis do that?"

"Believe me, *senor,* rigor mortis pounds upon no lids. Rigor mortis screams not like this, nor twists nor wrestles to rip free nails, *senor,* or prise boards loose hunting for air, *senor.* All these others are open of mouth, *si,* because they were not injected with the fluids of embalming, but theirs is a simple screaming of muscles, *senor.* This *senorita,* here, hers is the *muerte horrible.*"

Marie walked, scuffling her shoes, turning first this way, then that. Naked bodies. Long ago the clothes had whispered away. The fat women's breasts were lumps of yeasty dough left in the dust. The men's loins were indrawn, withered orchids.

"Mr. Grimace and Mr. Gape," said Joseph.

He pointed his camera at two men who seemed in conversation, mouths in mid-sentence, hands gesticulant and stiffened over some long-dissolved gossip.

Joseph clicked the shutter, rolled the film, focused the camera on another body, clicked the shutter, rolled the film, walked on to another.

Eighty-one, eighty-two, eighty-three. Jaws down, tongues out like jeering children, eyes pale brown-irised in upclenched sockets. Hairs, waxed and prickled by sunlight, each sharp as quills embedded on the lips, the cheeks, the eyelids, the brows. Little beards on chins and bosoms and loins. Flesh like drumheads and manuscripts and crisp bread dough. The women, huge ill-shaped tallow things, death-melted. The insane hair of them, like nests made and unmade and remade. Teeth, each single, each fine, each perfect, in jaw. Eighty-six, eighty-seven, eighty-eight. A rushing of Marie's eyes. Down the corridor, flicking. Counting, rushing, never stopping. On! Quick! Ninety-one, ninety-two, ninety-three! Here was a man, his stomach open, like a tree hollow where you dropped your child love letters when you were eleven! Her eyes entered the hole in the space under his ribs. She peeked in. He looked like an Erector set inside. The spine, the pelvic plates. The rest was tendon, parchment, bone, eye, beardy jaw, ear, stupefied nostril. And this ragged eaten cincture in his navel into which a pudding might be spooned. Ninety-seven, ninety-eight! Names, places, dates, things!

"This woman died in childbirth!"

Like a little hungry doll, the prematurely born child was wired, dangling, to her wrist.

"This was a soldier. His uniform still half on him——"

Marie's eyes slammed the furthest wall after a back-forth, back-forth swinging from horror to horror, from skull to skull, beating from rib to rib, staring with hypnotic fascination at paralyzed, loveless, fleshless loins, at men made into women by evaporation, at women made into dugged swine. The fearful ricochet of vision, growing, growing, taking impetus from swollen breast to raving mouth, wall to wall, wall to wall, again, again, like a ball hurled in a game, caught in the incredible teeth, spat in a scream across the corridor to be caught in claws, lodged between thin teats, the whole standing chorus invisibly chanting the game on, on, the wild game of sight recoiling, rebounding, reshuttling on down the inconceivable procession, through a montage of erected horrors that ended finally and for all time when vision crashed against the corridor ending with one last scream from all present!

Marie turned and shot her vision far down to where the spiral steps walked up into sunlight. How talented was death. How many expressions and manipulations of hand, face, body, no two alike. They stood like the naked pipes of a vast derelict calliope, their mouths cut into frantic vents. And now the great hand of mania descended upon all keys at once, and the long calliope screamed upon one hundred-throated, unending scream.

Click went the camera and Joseph rolled the film. Click went the camera and Joseph rolled the film.

Moreno, Morelos, Cantine, Gomez, Gutierrez, Villanousul, Ureta, Licon, Navarro, Iturbi; Jorge, Filomena, Nena, Manuel, Jose, Tomas, Ramona. This man walked and this man sang and this man had three wives; and this man died of this, and that of that, and the third from another thing, and the fourth was shot, and the fifth was stabbed and the sixth fell straight down dead; and the seventh drank deep and died dead, and the eighth died in love, and the ninth fell from his horse, and the tenth coughed blood, and the eleventh stopped his heart, and the twelfth used to laugh much, and the thirteenth was a dancing one, and the fourteenth was most beautiful of all, the fifteenth had ten children and the sixteenth is one of those children as is the seventeenth; and the eighteenth was Tomas and did well with his guitar; the next three cut maize in their fields, had three lovers each; the twenty-second was never loved; the twenty-third sold tortillas, patting and shaping them each at the curb before the Opera House with her little charcoal stove; and the twenty-fourth beat his wife and now she walks proudly in the town and is merry with new men and here he stands bewildered by this unfair thing, and the twenty-fifth drank several quarts of river with his lungs and was pulled forth in a net, and the twenty-sixth was a great thinker and his brain now sleeps like a burnt plum in his skull.

"I'd like a color shot of each, and his or her name and how he or she died," said Joseph. "It would be an amazing, an ironical book to publish. The more you think, the more it grows on you. Their life histories and then a picture of each of them standing here."

He tapped each chest, softly. They gave off hollow sounds, like someone rapping on a door.

Marie pushed her way through screams that hung netwise across her path. She walked evenly, in the corridor center, not slow, but not too fast, toward the spiral stair, not looking to either side. Click went the camera behind her.

"You have room down here for more?" said Joseph.

"Si, senor. Many more."

"Wouldn't want to be next in line, next on your waiting list."

"Ah, no, *senor,* one would not wish to be next."

"How are chances of buying one of these?"

"Oh, no, no, *senor.* Oh, no, no. Oh no, *senor.*"

"I'll pay you fifty pesos."

"Oh, no, *senor,* no, no, *senor.*"

In the market, the remainder of candy skulls from the Death Fiesta were sold from flimsy little tables. Women hung with black rebozos sat quietly, now and then speaking one word to each other, the sweet sugar skeletons, the saccharine corpses and white candy skulls at their elbows. Each skull had a name on top in gold candy curlicue; Jose or Carmen or Ramon or Tena or Guiermo or Rosa. They sold cheap. The Death Festival was gone. Joseph paid a peso and got two candy skulls.

Marie stood in the narrow street. She saw the candy skulls and Joseph and the dark ladies who put the skulls in a bag.

"Not *really,*" said Marie.

"Why not?" said Joseph.

"Not after just *now,*" she said.

"In the catacombs?"

She nodded.

He said, "But these are good."

"They look poisonous."

"Just because they're skull-shaped?"

"No. The sugar itself looks raw, how do you know what kind of people made them, they might have the colic."

"My dear Marie, all people in Mexico have colic," he said.

"You can eat them both," she said.

"Alas, poor Yorick," he said, peeking into the bag.

They walked along a street that was held between high buildings in which were yellow window frames and pink iron grilles and the smell of tamales came from them and the sound of lost fountains splashing on hidden tiles and little birds clustering and peeping in bamboo cages and someone playing Chopin on a piano.

"Chopin, here," said Joseph. "How strange and swell." He looked up. "I like that bridge. Hold this." He handed her the candy bag while he clicked a picture of a red bridge spanning two white buildings with a man walking on it, a red serape on his shoulder. "Fine," said Joseph.

Marie walked looking at Joseph, looking away from him and then back at him, her lips moving but not speaking, her eyes fluttering, a little neck muscle under her chin like a wire, a little nerve in her brow ticking. She passed the candy bag from one hand to the other. She stepped up a curb, leaned back somehow, gestured, said something to restore balance, and dropped the bag.

"For Christ's sake." Joseph snatched up the bag. "Look what you've done! Clumsy!"

"I should have broken my ankle," she said, "I suppose."

"These were the best skulls; both of them smashed; I wanted to save them for friends up home."

"I'm sorry," she said, vaguely.

"For God's sake, oh, damn it to hell." He scowled into the bag. "I might not find any more good as these. Oh, I don't know, I give up!"

The wind blew and they were alone in the street, he staring down into the shattered debris in the bag, she with the street shadows all around her, sun on the other side of the street, nobody about, and the world far away, the two of them alone, two thousand miles from anywhere, on a street in a false town behind which was nothing and around which was nothing but blank desert and circled hawks. On top the State Opera House, a block down, the golden Greek statues stood sun-bright and high, and in a beer place a shouting phonograph cried AY, MARIMBA . . . *corazon* . . . and all kinds of alien words which the wind stirred away.

Joseph twisted the bag shut, stuck it furiously in his pocket.

They walked back to the two-thirty lunch at the hotel.

He sat at the table with Marie, sipping Albondigas soup from his moving spoon, silently. Twice she commented cheerfully upon the wall murals and he looked at her steadily and sipped. The bag of cracked skulls lay on the table. . . .

"*Senora* . . ."

The soup plates were cleared by a brown hand. A large plate of *enchiladas* was set down.

Marie looked at the plate.

There were sixteen *enchiladas*.

She put her fork and knife out to take one and stopped. She put her fork and knife down at each side of her plate. She glanced at the walls and then ..t her husband and then at the sixteen *enchiladas*.

Sixteen. One by one. A long row of them, crowded together.

She counted them.

One, two, three, four, five, six.

Joseph took one on his plate and ate it.

Six, seven, eight, nine, ten, eleven.

She put her hands on her lap.

Twelve, thirteen, fourteen, fifteen, sixteen. She finished counting.

"I'm not hungry," she said.

He placed another *enchilada* before himself. It had an interior clothed in a papyrus of corn *tortilla*. It was slender and it was one of many he cut and placed in his mouth and she chewed it for him in her mind's mouth, and squeezed her eyes tight.

"Eh?" he asked.

"Nothing," she said.

Thirteen *enchiladas* remained, like tiny bundles, like scrolls.

He ate five more.

"I don't feel well," she said.

"Feel better if you ate," he said.

"No."

He finished, then opened the sack and took out one of the half-demolished skulls.

"Not *here?*" she said.

"Why not?" And he put one sugar socket to his lips, chewing. "Not bad," he said, thinking the taste. He popped in another section of skull. "Not bad at all."

She looked at the name on the skull he was eating.

Marie, it said.

It was tremendous, the way she helped him pack. In those newsreels you see men leap off diving-boards into pools, only, a moment later when the reel is reversed, to jump back up in airy fantasy to alight once more safe on the diving-board. Now, as Joseph watched, the suits and dresses flew into their boxes and cases, the hats were like birds darting, clapped into round, bright hatboxes, the shoes seemed to run across the floor like mice to leap into valises. The suitcases banged shut, the hasps clicked, the keys turned.

"There!" she cried. "All packed! Oh, Joe, I'm so glad you let me change your mind."

She started for the door.

"Here, let me help," he said.

"They're not heavy," she said.

"But you never carry suitcases. You never have. I'll call a boy."

"Nonsense," she said, breathless with the weight of the valises.

A boy seized the cases outside the door. *"Senora, por favor!"*

"Have we forgotten anything?" He looked under the two beds, he went out on the balcony and gazed at the plaza, came in, went to the bathroom, looked in the cabinet and on the washbowl. "Here," he said, coming out and handing her something. "You forgot your wrist watch."

"Did I?" She put it on and went out the door.

"I don't know," he said. "It's damn late in the day to be moving out."

"It's only three-thirty," she said. "Only three-thirty."

"I don't know," he said, doubtfully.

He looked around the room, stepped out, closed the door, locked it, went downstairs, jingling the keys.

She was outside in the car already, settled in, her coat folded on her lap, her gloved hands folded on the coat. He came out, supervised the loading of what luggage remained into the trunk receptacle, came to the front door and tapped on the window. She unlocked it and let him in.

"Well, here we *go!*" She cried with a laugh, her face rosy, her eyes franticaliy bright. She was leaning forward as if by this movement she might set the car rolling merrily down the hill. "Thank you, darling, for letting me get the refund on the money you paid for our room tonight. I'm sure we'll like it much better in Guadalajara tonight. Thank you!"

"Yeah," he said.

Inserting the ignition keys he stepped on the starter.

Nothing happened.

He stepped on the starter again. Her mouth twitched.

"It needs warming," she said. "It was a cold night last night."

He tried it again. Nothing.

Marie's hands tumbled on her lap.

He tried it six more times. "Well," he said, lying back, ceasing.

"Try it again, next time it'll work," she said.

"It's no use," he said. "Something's wrong."

"Well, you've got to try it once more."

He tried it once more.

"It'll work, I'm sure," she said. "Is the ignition on?"

"Is the ignition on," he said. "Yes, it's *on.*"

"It doesn't look like it's on," she said.

"It's on." He showed her by twisting the key.

"*Now,* try it," she said.

"There," he said, when nothing happened. "I *told* you."

"You're not doing it right; it almost caught that time," she cried.

"I'll wear out the battery, and God knows where you can buy a battery here."

"Wear it out, then. I'm sure it'll start next time!"

"Well, if you're so good, you try it." He slipped from the car and beckoned her over behind the wheel. "Go ahead!"

She bit her lips and settled behind the wheel. She did

things with her hands that were like a little mystic ceremony; with moves of hands and body she was trying to overcome gravity, friction and every other natural law. She patted the starter with her toeless shoe. The car remained solemnly quiet. A little squeak came out of Marie's tightened lips. She rammed the starter home and there was a clear smell in the air as she fluttered the choke.

"You've flooded it," he said. "Fine! Get back over on your side, will you?"

He got three boys to push and they started the car downhill. He jumped in to steer. The car rolled swiftly, bumping and rattling. Marie's face glowed expectantly. "This'll start it!" she said.

Nothing started. They rolled quietly into the filling station at the bottom of the hill, bumping softly on the cobbles, and stopped by the tanks.

She sat there, saying nothing, and when the attendant came from the station her door was locked, the window up, and he had to come around on the husband's side to make his query.

The mechanic arose from the car engine, scowled at Joseph and they spoke together in Spanish, quietly.

She rolled the window down and listened.

"What's he say?" she demanded.

The two men talked on.

"What does he say?" she asked.

The dark mechanic waved at the engine. Joseph nodded and they conversed.

"What's wrong?" Marie wanted to know.

Joseph frowned over at her. "Wait a moment, will you? I can't listen to both of you."

The mechanic took Joseph's elbow. They said many words.

"What's he saying now?" she asked.

"He says——" said Joseph, and was lost as the Mexican took him over to the engine and bent him down in earnest discovery.

"How much will it cost?" she cried, out the window, around at their bent backs.

The mechanic spoke to Joseph.

"Fifty pesos," said Joseph.

"How long will it take?" cried his wife.

Joseph asked the mechanic. The man shrugged and they argued for five minutes.

"How long will it take?" said Marie.

The discussion continued.

The sun went down the sky. She looked at the sun upon the trees that stood high by the cemetery yard. The shadows rose and rose until the valley was enclosed and only the sky was clear and untouched and blue.

"Two days, maybe three," said Joseph, turning to Marie.

"Two days! Can't he fix it so we can just go on to the next town and have the rest done there?"

Joseph asked the man. The man replied.

Joseph said to his wife. "No, he'll have to do the entire job."

"Why, that's silly, it's so silly, he doesn't either, he doesn't really have to do it all, you tell him that, Joe, tell him that, he can hurry and fix it——"

The two men ignored her. They were talking earnestly again.

This time it was all in very slow motion. The unpacking of the suitcases. He did his own, she left hers by the door.

"I don't need anything," she said, leaving it locked.

"You'll need your nightgown," he said.

"I'll sleep naked," she said.

"Well, it isn't my fault," he said. "That damned car."

"You can go down and watch them work on it, later," she said. She sat on the edge of the bed. They were in a new room. She had refused to return to their old room. She said she couldn't stand it. She wanted a new room so it would seem they were in a new hotel in a new city. So this was a new room, with a view of the alley and the sewer system instead of the plaza and the drum-box trees. "You go down and supervise the work, Joe. If you don't, you know they'll take weeks!" She looked at him. "You should be down there now, instead of standing around."

"I'll go down," he said.

"I'll go down with you. I want to buy some magazines."

"You won't find any American magazines in a town like this."

"I can look, can't I?"

"Besides, we haven't much money," he said. "I don't want to have to wire my bank. It takes a god-awful time and it's not worth the bother."

"I can at least have my magazines," she said.

"Maybe one or two," he said.

"As many as I want," she said, feverishly, on the bed.

"For God's sake, you've got a million magazines in the car now, *Posts, Collier's, Mercury, Atlantic Monthlys, Barnaby, Superman!* You haven't read half of the articles."

"But they're not new," she said. "They're not new, I've *looked* at them and after you've looked at a thing, I don't know——"

"Try reading them instead of looking at them," he said.

As they came downstairs night was in the plaza.

"Give me a few pesos," she said, and he gave her some. "Teach me to say about magazines in Spanish," she said.

"*Quiero una publicacion Americano,*" he said, walking swiftly.

She repeated it, stumblingly, and laughed. "Thanks."

He went on ahead to the mechanic's shop, and she turned in at the nearest *Farmacia Botica,* and all the magazines racked before her there were alien colors and alien names. She read the titles with swift moves of her eyes and looked at the old man behind the counter. "Do you have American magazines?" she asked in English, embarrassed to use the Spanish words.

The old man stared at her.

"*Habla Ingles?*" she asked.

"No, *senorita.*"

She tried to think of the right words. "*Quiero*—no!" She stopped. She started again. "*Americano*—uh—*magg-ah-zeen-as?*"

"Oh, no, *senorita!*"

Her hands opened wide at her waist, then closed, like mouths. Her mouth opened and closed. The shop had a veil over it, in her eyes. Here she was and here were these small baked adobe people to whom she could say nothing and from whom she could get no words she understood, and she was in a town of people who said no words to her and she said no words to them except in blushing confusion and bewilderment. And the town was circled by desert and time, and home was far away, far away in another life.

She whirled and fled.

Shop following shop she found no magazines save those giving bullfights in blood on their covers or murdered people or lace-confection priests. But at last three poor copies of the *Post* were bought with much display and loud laughter and she gave the vendor of this small shop a handsome tip.

Rushing out with the *Posts* eagerly on her bosom in both hands she hurried along the narrow walk, took a skip over the gutter, ran across the street, sang la-la, jumped onto the further walk, made another little scamper with her feet, smiled an inside smile, moving along swiftly, pressing the magazines tightly to her, half-closing her eyes, breathing the charcoal evening air, feeling the wind watering past her ears.

Starlight tinkled in golden nuclei off the highly perched Greek figures atop the State theatre. A man shambled by in the shadow, balancing upon his head a basket. The basket contained bread loaves.

She saw the man and the balanced basket and suddenly she did not move and there was no inside smile, nor did her hands clasp tight the magazines. She watched the man walk, with one hand of his gently poised up to tap the basket any time it unbalanced, and down the street he dwindled, while the magazines slipped from Marie's fingers and scattered on the walk.

Snatching them up, she ran into the hotel and almost fell going upstairs.

She sat in the room. The magazines were piled on each side of her and in a circle at her feet. She had made a little castle with portcullises of words and into this she was withdrawn. All about her were the magazines she had bought and bought and looked at and looked at on other days, and these were the outer barrier, and upon the inside of the barrier, upon her lap, as yet unopened, but her hands were trembling to open them and read and read and read again with hungry eyes, were the three battered *Post* magazines. She opened the first page. She would go through them page by page, line by line, she decided. Not a line would go unnoticed, a comma unread, every little ad and every color would be fixed by her. And—she smiled with discovery—in those other magazines at her feet were still advertisements and cartoons she had neglected—there would be little morsels of stuff for her to reclaim and utilize later.

She would read this first *Post* tonight, yes tonight she would read this first delicious *Post.* Page on page she would eat it and tomorrow night, if there was going to be a tomorrow night, but maybe there wouldn't be a tomorrow night here, maybe the motor would start and there'd be odors of exhaust and round hum of rubber tire on road and wind riding in the window and pennanting her hair—but, suppose, just suppose there would BE a tomorrow night here, in this room. Well, then, there would be two more *Posts,* one for tomorrow night, and the next for the next night. How neatly she said it to herself with her mind's tongue. She turned the first page.

She turned the second page. Her eyes moved over it and over it and her fingers unknown to her slipped under the next page and flickered it in preparation for turning, and the watch ticked on her wrist, and time passed and she sat turning pages, turning pages, hungrily seeing the framed people in the pictures, people who lived in another land in another world where neons bravely held off the night with crimson bars and the smells were home smells and the people talked good fine words and here she was turning the pages, and all the lines went across and down and the pages flew under her hands, making a fan. She threw down the first *Post,* seized on and riffled through the second in half an hour, threw that down, took up the third, threw that down a good fifteen minutes later and found herself breathing, breathing stiffly and swiftly in her body and out of her mouth. She put her hand up to the back of her neck.

Somewhere, a soft breeze was blowing.

The hairs along the back of her neck slowly stood upright.

She touched them with one pale hand as one touches the nape of a dandelion.

Outside, in the plaza, the street lights rocked like crazy flashlights on a wind. Papers ran through the gutters in sheep flocks. Shadows penciled and slashed under the bucketing lamps now this way, now that, here a shadow one instant, there a shadow next, now no shadows, all cold light, now no light, all cold blue-black shadow. The lamps creaked on their high metal hasps.

In the room her hands began to tremble. She saw them tremble. Her body began to tremble. Under the bright bright print of the brightest, loudest skirt she could find to put on especially for tonight, in which she had whirled and cavorted feverishly before the coffin-sized mirror, beneath the rayon skirt the body was all wire and tendon and excitation. Her teeth chattered and fused and chattered. Her lipstick smeared, one lip crushing another.

Joseph knocked on the door.

They got ready for bed. He had returned with the news that something had been done to the car and it would take time, he'd go watch them tomorrow.

"But don't knock on the door," she said, standing before the mirror as she undressed.

"Leave it unlocked then," he said.

"I want it locked. But don't rap. Call."

"What's wrong with rapping?" he said.

"It sounds funny," she said.

"What do you mean, funny?"

She wouldn't say. She was looking at herself in the mirror and she was naked, with her hands at her sides, and there were her breasts and her hips and her entire body, and it moved, it felt the floor under it and the walls and air around it, and the breasts could know hands if hands were put there, and the stomach would make no hollow echo if touched.

"For God's sake," he said, "don't stand there admiring

yourself." He was in bed. "What are you doing?" he said. "What're you putting your hands up that way for, over your face?"

He put the lights out.

She could not speak to him for she knew no words that he knew and he said nothing to her that she understood, and she walked to her bed and slipped into it and he lay with his back to her in his bed and he was like one of these brown-baked people of this far-away town upon the moon, and the real earth was off somewhere where it would take a star-flight to reach it. If only he could speak with her and she to him tonight, how good the night might be, and how easy to breathe and how lax the vessels of blood in her ankles and in her wrists and the under-arms, but there was no speaking and the night was ten thousand tickings and ten thousand twistings of the blankets, and the pillow was like a tiny white warm stove under-cheek, and the blackness of the room was a mosquito netting draped all about so that a turn entangled her in it. If only there was one word, one word between them. But there was no word and the veins did not rest easy in the wrists and the heart was a bellows forever blowing upon a little coal of fear, forever illumining and making it into a cherry light, again, pulse, and again, an ingrown light which her inner eyes stared upon with unwanting fascination. The lungs did not rest but were exercised as if she were a drowned person and she herself performing artificial respiration to keep the last life going. And all of these things were lubricated by the sweat of her glowing body, and she was glued fast between the heavy blankets like something pressed, smashed, redolently moist between the white pages of a heavy book.

And as she lay this way the long hours of midnight came when again she was a child. She lay, now and again thumping her heart in tambourine hysteria, then, quieting, the slow sad thoughts of bronze childhood when everything was sun on green trees and sun on water and sun on blond child hair. Faces flowed by on merry-go-rounds of memory, a face rushing to meet her, facing her, and away to the right; another, whirling in from the left, a quick fragment of lost conversation, and out to the right. Around and round. Oh, the night was very long. She consoled herself by thinking of the car starting tomorrow, the throttling sound and the power sound and the road moving under, and she smiled in the dark with pleasure. But then, suppose the car did *not* start? She crumpled in the dark, like a burning, withering paper. All the folds and corners of her clenched in about her and tick tick tick went the wristwatch, tick tick tick and another tick to wither on. . . .

Morning. She looked at her husband lying straight and easy on his bed. She let her hand laze down at the cool space between the beds. All night her hand had hung in that cold empty interval between. Once she had put her hand out toward him, stretching, but the space was just a little too long, she couldn't reach him. She had snapped her hand back, hoping he hadn't heard the movement of her silent reaching.

There he lay now. His eyes gently closed, the lashes softly interlocked like clasped fingers. Breathing so quietly you could scarce see his ribs move. As usual, by this time of morning, he had worked out of his pajamas. His naked chest was revealed from the waist up. The rest of him lay under cover. His head lay on the pillow, in thoughtful profile.

There was a beard stubble on his chin.

The morning light showed the white of her eyes. They were the only things in the room in motion, in slow starts and stops, tracing the anatomy of the man across from her.

Each little hair was perfect on the chin and cheeks. A tiny hole of sunlight from the window-shade lay on his chin and picked out, like the spikes of a music-box cylinder, each little hair on his face.

His wrists on either side of him had little curly black hairs, each perfect, each separate and shiny and glittering.

The hair on his head was intact, strand by dark strand, down to the roots. The ears were beautifully carved. The teeth were intact behind the lips.

"Joseph!" she screamed.

"Joseph!" she screamed again, flailing up in terror.

Bong! Bong! Bong! went the bell thunder across the street, from the great tiled cathedral!

Pigeons rose in a papery white whirl, like so many magazines fluttered past the window! The pigeons circled the plaza, spiraling up. Bong! went the bells! Honk went a taxi horn! Far away down an alley a music box played "Cielito Lindo."

All these faded into the dripping of the faucet in the bath sink.

Joseph opened his eyes.

His wife sat on her bed, staring at him.

"I thought—" he said. He blinked. "No." He shut his eyes and shook his head. "Just the bells." A sigh. "What time is it?"

"I don't know. Yes, I do. Eight o'clock."

"Good God," he murmured, turning over. "We can sleep three more hours."

"You've got to get up!" she cried.

"Nobody's up. They won't be to work at the garage until ten, you know that, you can't rush these people; keep quiet now."

"But you've got to get up," she said.

He half-turned. Sunlight prickled black hairs into bronze on his upper lip. *"Why?* Why, in Christ's name, do I *have* to get up?"

"You need a shave!" she almost screamed.

He moaned. "So I have to get up and lather myself at eight in the morning because I need a shave."

"Well, you do need one."

"I'm not shaving again till we reach Texas."

"You can't go around looking like a tramp!"

"I can and will. I've shaved every morning for thirty god-damn mornings and put on a tie and had a crease in my pants. From now on, no pants, no ties, no shaving, no nothing."

He yanked the covers over his ears so violently that he pulled the blankets off one of his naked legs.

The leg hung upon the rim of the bed, warm white in the sunlight, each little black hair—perfect.

Her eyes widened, focused, stared upon it.
She put her hand over her mouth, tight.

He went in and out of the hotel all day. He did not
shave. He walked along the plaza tiles below. He walked so
slowly she wanted to throw a lightning bolt out of the window and hit him. He paused and talked to the hotel man-
ager below, under a drum-cut tree, shifting his shoes on
the pale blue plaza tiles. He looked at birds on trees and
saw how the State Theatre statues were dressed in fresh
morning gilt, and stood on the corner, watching the traffic
carefully. There was no traffic! He was standing there on
purpose, taking his time, not looking back at her. Why
didn't he run, lope down the alley, down the hill to the
garage, pound on the doors, threaten the mechanics, lift
them by their pants, shove them into the car motor! He
stood instead, watching the ridiculous traffic pass. A hob-
bled swine, a man on a bike, a 1927 Ford, and three half-
nude children. Go, go, go, she screamed silently, and almost
smashed the window.

He sauntered across the street. He went around the corner. All the way down to the garage he'd stop at windows,
read signs, look at pictures, handle pottery. Maybe he'd
stop in for a beer. God, yes, a beer.

She walked in the plaza, took the sun, hunted for more
magazines. She cleaned her fingernails, burnished them,
took a bath, walked again in the plaza, ate very little, and
returned to the room to feed upon her magazines.

She did not lie down. She was afraid to. Each time she
did she fell into a half-dream, half-drowse in which all her
childhood was revealed in a helpless melancholy. Old
friends, children she hadn't seen or thought of in twenty
years filled her mind. And she thought of things she wanted
to do and had never done. She had meant to call Lila Hol-
dridge for the past eight years since college, but somehow
she never had. What friends they had been! Dear Lila! She
thought, when lying down, of all the books, the fine new
and old books, she had meant to buy and might never buy
now and read. How she loved books and the smell of books.
She thought of a thousand old sad things. She'd wanted to

own the Oz books all her life, yet had never bought them. Why *not?* while yet there was life! The first thing she'd do would be to buy them when she got back to New York! And she'd call Lila immediately! And she'd see Bert and Jimmy and Helen and Louise, and go back to Illinois and walk around in her childhood place and see the things to be seen there. If she got back to the States. If. Her heart beat painfully in her, paused, held on to itself, and beat again. *If* she ever got back.

She lay listening to her heart, critically.

Thud and a thud and a thud. Pause. Thud and a thud and a thud. Pause.

What if it should stop while she was listening?

There!

Silence inside her.

"Joseph!"

She leaped up. She grabbed at her breasts as if to squeeze, to pump to start the silent heart again!

It opened in her, closed, rattled and beat nervously, twenty rapid, shot-like times!

She sank on to the bed. What if it should stop again and not start? What would she think? What would there be to do? She'd die of fright, that's what. A joke; it was very humorous. Die of fright if you heard your heart stop. She would have to listen to it, keep it beating. She wanted to go home and see Lila and buy the books and dance again and walk in Central Park and—listen—

Thud and a thud and a thud. Pause.

Joseph knocked on the door. Joseph knocked on the door and the car was not repaired and there would be another night, and Joseph did not shave and each little hair was perfect on his chin, and the magazine shops were closed and there were no more magazines, and they ate supper, a little bit anyway for her, and he went out in the evening to walk in the town.

She sat once more in the chair and slow erections of hair rose as if a magnet were passed over her neck. She was very weak and could not move from the chair, and she had no body, she was only a heart-beat, a huge pulsation of warmth and ache between four walls of the room. Her eyes were hot and pregnant, swollen with child of terror behind the bellied, tautened lids.

Deeply inside herself, she felt the first little cog slip. Another night, another night, another night, she thought. And this will be longer than the last. The first little cog slipped, the pendulum missed a stroke. Followed by the second and third interrelated cogs. The cogs interlocked, a small with a little larger one, the little larger one with a bit larger one, the bit larger one with a large one, the large one with a huge one, the huge one with an immense one, the immense one with a titanic one. . . .

A red ganglion, no bigger than a scarlet thread, snapped and quivered; a nerve, no greater than a red linen fiber twisted. Deep in her one little mesh was gone and the entire machine, imbalanced, was about to steadily shake itself to bits.

She didn't fight it. She let it quake and terrorize her and knock the sweat off her brow and jolt down her spine and flood her mouth with horrible wine. She felt as if a broken gyro tilted now this way, now that and blundered and trembled and whined in her. The color fell from her face like light leaving a clicked-off bulb, the crystal cheeks of the bulb vessel showing veins and filaments all colorless. . . .

Joseph was in the room, he had come in, but she didn't even hear him. He was in the room but it made no difference, he changed nothing with his coming. He was getting ready for bed and said nothing as he moved about and she said nothing but fell into the bed while he moved around in a smoke-filled space beyond her and once he spoke but she didn't hear him.

She timed it. Every five minutes she looked at her watch and the watch shook and time shook and the five fingers were fifteen moving, reassembling into five. The shaking never stopped. She called for water. She turned and turned upon the bed. The wind blew outside, cocking the lights and spilling bursts of illumination that hit buildings glancing sidelong blows, causing windows to glitter like opened eyes and shut swiftly as the light tilted in yet another direction.

Downstairs, all was quiet after the dinner, no sounds came up into their silent room. He handed her a water glass.

"I'm cold, Joseph," she said, lying deep in folds of cover.

"You're all right," he said.

"No, I'm not. I'm not well. I'm afraid."

"There's nothing to be afraid of."

"I want to get on the train for the United States."

"There's a train in Leon, but none here," he said, lighting a new cigarette.

"Let's drive there."

"In these taxis, with these drivers, and leave our car here?"

"Yes. I want to go."

"You'll be all right in the morning."

"I know I won't be. I'm not well."

He said, "It would cost hundreds of dollars to have the car shipped home."

"I don't care. I have two hundred dollars in the bank home. I'll pay for it. But, please, let's go home."

"When the sun shines tomorrow you'll feel better, it's just that the sun's gone now."

"Yes, the sun's gone and the wind's blowing," she whispered, closing her eyes, turning her head, listening. "Oh, what a lonely wind. Mexico's a strange land. All the jungles and deserts and lonely stretches, and here and there a little town, like this, with a few lights burning you could put out with a snap of your fingers . . ."

"It's a pretty big country," he said.

"Don't these people ever get lonely?"

"They're used to it this way."

"Don't they get afraid, then?"

"They have a religion for that."

"I wish *I* had a religion."

"The minute you get a religion you stop thinking," he said. "Believe in one thing too much and you have no room for new ideas."

"Tonight," she said, faintly. "I'd like nothing more than to have no more room for new ideas, to stop thinking, to believe in one thing so much it leaves me no time to be afraid."

"You're not afraid," he said.

"If I had a religion," she said, ignoring him, "I'd have a lever with which to lift myself. But I haven't a lever now and I don't know how to lift myself."

"Oh, for God's—" he mumbled to himself, sitting down.

"I used to have a religion," she said.

"Baptist."

"No, that was when I was twelve. I got over that. I mean —later."

"You never told me."

"You should have known," she said.

"What religion? Plaster saints in the sacristy? Any special special saint you liked to tell your beads to?"

"Yes."

"And did he answer your prayers?"

"For a little while. Lately, no, never. Never any more. Not for years now. But I keep praying."

"Which saint is this?"

"Saint Joseph."

"Saint Joseph." He got up and poured himself a glass of water from the glass pitcher, and it was a lonely trickling sound in the room. "My name."

"Coincidence," she said.

They looked at one another for a few moments.

He looked away. "Plaster saints," he said, drinking the water down.

After a while she said, "Joseph?" He said, "Yes?" and she said, "Come hold my hand, will you?" "Women," he sighed. He came and held her hand. After a minute she drew her hand away, hid it under the blanket, leaving his hand empty behind. With her eyes closed she trembled the words, "Never mind. It's not as nice as I can imagine it. It's really nice the way I can make you hold my hand in my mind." "Gods," he said, and went into the bathroom. She turned off the light. Only the small crack of light under the bathroom door showed. She listened to her heart. It beat one hundred and fifty times a minute, steadily, and the little whining tremor was still in her marrow, as if each bone of her body had a blue-bottle fly imprisoned in it, hovering, buzzing, shaking, quivering deep, deep, deep. Her eyes reversed into herself, to watch the secret heart of herself pounding itself to pieces against the side of her chest.

Water ran in the bathroom. She heard him washing his teeth.

"Joseph!"

"Yes," he said, behind the shut door.

"Come here."

"What do you want?"

"I want you to promise me something, please, oh, please."

"What is it?"

"Open the door, first."

"What *is* it?" he demanded, behind the closed door.

"Promise me," she said, and stopped.

"Promise you what?" he asked, after a long pause.

"Promise me," she said, and couldn't go on. She lay there. He said nothing. She heard the watch and her heart pounding together. A lantern creaked on the hotel exterior. "Promise me, if anything—happens," she heard herself say, muffled and paralyzed, as if she were on one of the surrounding hills talking at him from the distance, "—if anything happens to me, you won't let me be buried here in the graveyard over those terrible catacombs!"

"Don't be foolish," he said, behind the door.

"Promise me?" she said, eyes wide in the dark.

"Of all the foolish things to talk about."

"Promise, *please* promise?"

"You'll be all right in the morning," he said.

"Promise so I can sleep. I can sleep if only you'd say you wouldn't let me be put there. I don't want to be put there."

"Honestly," he said, out of patience.

"Please," she said.

"Why should I promise anything so ridiculous?" he said. "You'll be fine tomorrow. And besides, if you died, you'd look very pretty in the catacomb standing between Mr. Grimace and Mr. Gape, with a sprig of morning-glory in your hair." And he laughed sincerely.

Silence. She lay there in the dark.

"Don't you think you'll look pretty there?" he asked, laughingly, behind the door.

She said nothing in the dark room.

"*Don't* you?" he said.

Somebody walked down below in the plaza, faintly, fading away.

"Eh?" he asked her, brushing his teeth.

She lay there, staring up at the ceiling, her breast rising and falling faster, faster, faster, the air going in and out, in and out her nostrils, a little trickle of blood coming from her clenched lips. Her eyes were very wide, her hands blindly constricted the bedclothes.

"Eh?" he said again behind the door.

She said nothing.

"Sure," he talked to himself. "Pretty as hell," he murmured, under the flow of tap water. He rinsed his mouth. "Sure," he said.

Nothing from her in the bed.

"Women are funny," he said to himself in the mirror.

She lay in the bed.

"Sure," he said. He gargled with some antiseptic, spat it down the drain. "You'll be all right in the morning," he said.

Not a word from her.

"We'll get the car fixed."

She didn't say anything.

"Be morning before you know it." He was screwing caps on things now, putting freshener on his face. "And the car fixed tomorrow, maybe, at the very latest the next day. You won't mind another night here, will you?"

She didn't answer.

"*Will* you?" he asked.

No reply.

The light blinked out under the bathroom door.

"Marie?"

He opened the door.

"Asleep?"

She lay with eyes wide, breasts moving up and down.

"Asleep," he said. "Well, good night, lady."

He climbed into his bed. "Tired," he said.

No reply.

"Tired," he said.

The wind tossed the lights outside; the room was oblong and black and he was in his bed dozing already.

She lay, eyes wide, the watch ticking on her wrist, breasts moving up and down.

It was a fine day coming through the Tropic of Cancer. The automobile pushed along the turning road leaving the jungle country behind, heading for the United States, roaring between the green hills, taking every turn, leaving behind a faint vanishing trail of exhaust smoke. And inside the shiny automobile sat Joseph with his pink, healthy face and his Panama hat, and a little camera cradled on his lap as he drove; a swathe of black silk pinned around the left upper arm of his tan coat. He watched the country slide by and absent-mindedly made a gesture to the seat beside him, and stopped. He broke into a little sheepish smile and turned once more to the window of his car, humming a tuneless tune, his right hand slowly reaching over to touch the seat beside him . . .

Which was empty.

THE MUMMIES

THE MUMMIES

THE MUMMIES

THE MUMMIES

THE MUMMIES

Archie Lieberman

THE MUMMIES
THE MUMMIES
THE MUMMIES
THE MUMMIES
THE MUMMIES
THE MUMMIES
THE MUMMIES
THE MUMMIES

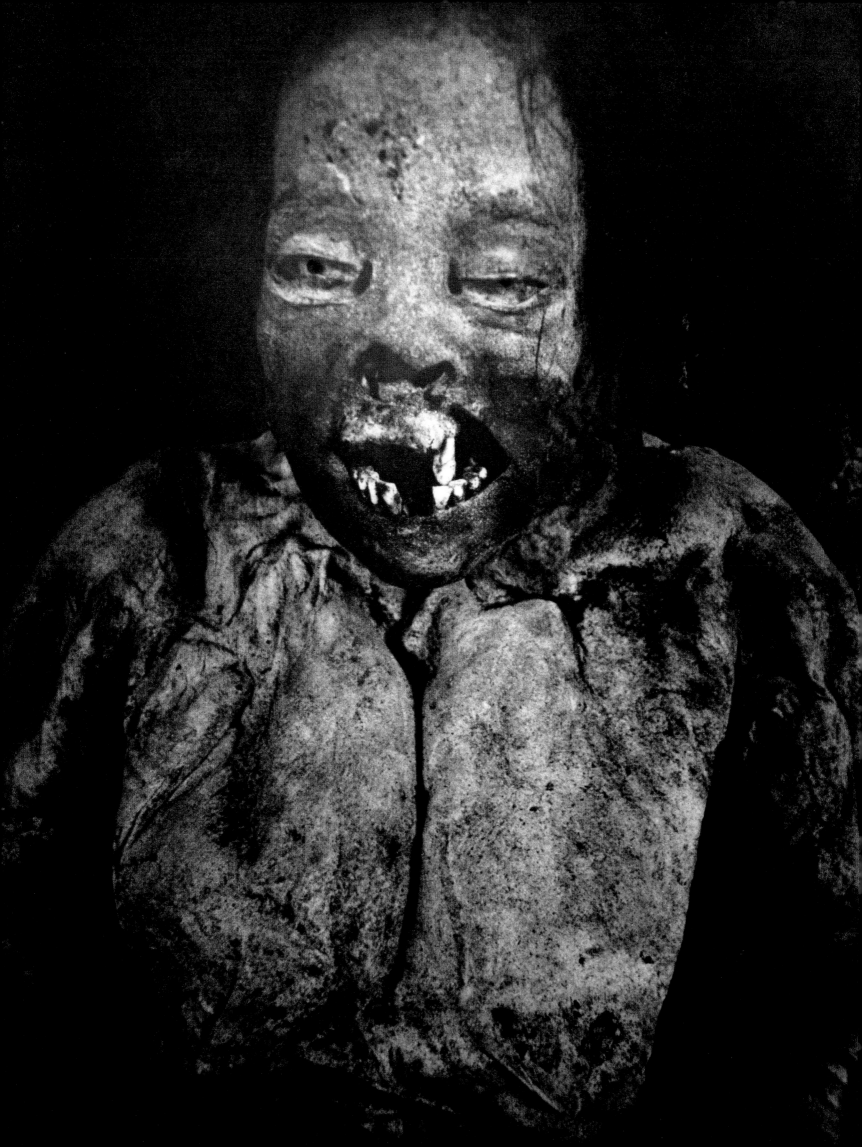

WE ARE SUCH STUFF
AS DREAMS ARE MADE ON
AND OUR LITTLE LIFE IS
ROUNDED WITH A
SLEEP